THE ROYAL RAVEN

HANS WILHELM

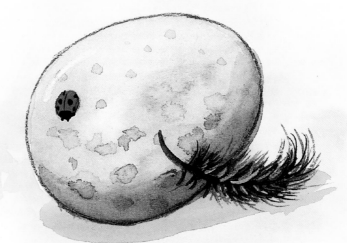

Cartwheel
·B·O·O·K·S·®

SCHOLASTIC INC.

New York   Toronto   London   Auckland   Sydney

To Sylvia Edwards

ISBN 0-590-54337-7

Copyright © 1996 by Hans Wilhelm, Inc.
All rights reserved. Published by Scholastic Inc.
CARTWHEEL BOOKS and the CARTWHEEL BOOKS logo
are registered trademarks of Scholastic Inc.

12 11 10 9 8 7 6 5 4 3 2 1   6 7 8 9/9 0 1/0
10

First Scholastic printing, March 1996
Printed in Hong Kong

*C*rack! The egg popped open and out came Crawford.
"Here I am!" he crowed.

But there was no reply. His mother was out looking for
food. He was all by himself. There was nobody to make a
fuss about his arrival.

Then came an even bigger disappointment.

Crawford saw that he was a boring-looking raven, like all the others.
Deep in his heart he felt he was special. He tried to show how different he was. "Look at me!" he said.

But nobody ever paid any attention.

At first Crawford was furious. That didn't help much. Then he began to feel sorry for himself. Every time he caught sight of his ordinary raven's feathers, he wished he looked different. "Why can't I look like a swan? Or a cardinal? Or an eagle? Or even like a silly little hummingbird? Anything would be better than this."

Thursday **Friday** **Saturday**

Every day Crawford came up with another idea to improve his appearance. But it was no use. Nothing seemed to be just right.

"I have to do something more drastic!" he said as he flew off into the deepest part of the forest.

There he called upon an old woman who was known for her special powers.

Crawford came right to the point: "I'll do anything for you if you can make me different. I want some color, some flash, some razzle dazzle!"

"What can a silly little raven like you do for me?" the old woman sneered. "You're no good at all." She paused.

"However ... " she went on, "I might use some of your tail feathers to spice up this brew."

"Done!" said Crawford. And he plucked out some of his longest tail feathers and gave them to the woman.

"Abracadabra, Shaloo-Kaloo, Shalee-Kalee!" croaked the old woman. And with a *bang*, a *boom*, a *zipp*, and a *zapp*, Crawford was transformed into a spectacular creature with dazzling, shiny feathers.

"Wow!" cried Crawford as he looked himself over.

"I hope I didn't overdo it," said the old woman.

Then, without even bothering to thank her, Crawford flew back to his friends.

"Look at me! Look at me!" he cried. He spread his wings and strutted up and down with his beak high in the air.

Who is this crazy bird? the other ravens wondered. But they were too polite to say anything.

"It's me! Crawford! Look how beautiful I am now!"

The other ravens just stared in silence.

"I'm special! I'm unique!" Crawford boasted. "Such beauty should not be hidden in a dark forest. The royal garden is the place for me!"

With that, he flew off to the king's castle.

As Crawford swooped around the royal garden, he was spotted by the princess.

"Look at that glorious bird!" she cried.

"Don't let it get away! I want it!"

Crawford was caught and tied to a golden chain.
Proudly the princess showed off her new treasure.
Crawford didn't mind in the least. After all, he was now
part of the royal family. What more could he have wished
for? He had it all: dazzling beauty, lots of attention, and
a wonderful place to live!

Unfortunately,
the royal raven's table
manners left much to be
desired. He lost a great deal
of his popularity when he caused
a major ruckus in the royal dining
room.

He was ordered OUT.

And the king made a decree banning
all birds from the dinner table — even those
that were roasted, broiled, or barbecued.

Crawford was banished to
a huge golden cage that stood
all alone in the royal garden.

Servants brought him food, but hardly anyone came to see him anymore. Once in a while somebody would pass by and say: "Oh, what a beautiful bird."

But this praise did not make him happy. Each day Crawford got sadder and sadder. He could see the other birds fly by, and he longed to join them. All he wanted was to be free again.

He lost his appetite and grew weaker and weaker.

One day an old woman came to the garden selling strawberries.

"What a sad-looking bird," the old woman said. "Why don't you let it go?"

"Oh, no," said the princess. "This bird is too precious. There isn't another in the whole kingdom with such dazzling feathers."

"Oh, I see," the old woman said. "So you keep him for his razzle dazzle."

Suddenly Crawford understood what he had to do to gain back his freedom.

He began to pluck out all
his beautiful feathers, one by one.
When the princess saw what he had
done, she screamed: "Get that horrid bird
out of my sight!"

That was exactly what Crawford wanted.
The guards opened the door of the cage. At last
Crawford was free again.

Crawford sure looked different now.
But he wasn't worried.

"My feathers will grow back," he said.
"And I don't care if they are gold, silver,
purple, striped, spotted, or just plain
black."

And neither did his friends.